MACMILLAN CHILDREN'S BOOKS

Hippo Has A Hat

Written by
Julia Donaldson

Illustrated by
Nick Sharratt

Lots of clothes! Let's try them.

Maybe we can buy them.

Tiger tries a shirt.

Leopard likes this skirt.

Hippo has a hat.

A cardigan for Cat.

Camel finds a coat.

An anorak for Goat.

Toad's tracksuit is too big.

These jeans are tight on Pig.

Zebra's zip has stuck.

"This can't be right!" says Duck.

Shoes for Caterpillar.

Slippers for Gorilla.

Flamingo buys a bag.

A string of beads for Stag.

Now everyone looks smart . . .

So let the party start!

For Tom
J.D.

For Henry
N.S.

First published 2006 by Macmillan Children's Books
a division of Macmillan Publishers Limited
20 New Wharf Road, London N1 9RR
Basingstoke and Oxford
Associated companies throughout the world
www.panmacmillan.com

ISBN - 13 : 978-1-4050-2191-3
ISBN - 10 : 1-4050-2191-8

Text copyright © Julia Donaldson 2006
Illustrations copyright © Nick Sharratt 2006